ETHAN LONG

PRESENTS

FRIGHT CLUB

BLOOMSBURY

NEW YORK   LONDON   NEW DELHI   SYDNEY

First published in the United States of America in August 2015 by Bloomsbury Children's Books
www.bloomsbury.com

Bloomsbury is a registered trademark of Bloomsbury Publishing Plc

For information about permission to reproduce selections from this book, write to Permissions, Bloomsbury Children's Books, 1385 Broadway, New York, New York 10018
Bloomsbury books may be purchased for business or promotional use. For information on bulk purchases please contact Macmillan Corporate and Premium Sales Department at
specialmarkets@macmillan.com

Library of Congress Cataloging-in-Publication Data
Long, Ethan, author, illustrator.
Fright Club / by Ethan Long.
pages   cm
Summary: As the monsters of the Fright Club prepare to scare children on Halloween, an adorable little bunny tries to join the club.
ISBN 978-1-61963-337-7 (hardcover)
ISBN 978-1-61963-418-3 (e-book) • ISBN 978-1-61963-419-0 (e-PDF)
[1. Halloween—Fiction. 2. Monsters—Fiction. 3. Clubs—Fiction.] I. Title.
PZ7.L8453Fr 2015   [E]—dc23   2014021459

Artwork created with graphite pencil on Strathmore drawing paper, then scanned and colorized digitally
Book design by Ethan Long and Yelena Safronova • Handlettering by Ethan Long; typeset in Sprocket BT

Printed in China by Leo Paper Products, Heshan, Guangdong
2 4 6 8 10 9 7 5 3 1

All papers used by Bloomsbury Publishing, Inc., are natural, recyclable products made from wood grown in well-managed
forests. The manufacturing processes conform to the environmental regulations of the country of origin.

To all my friends in dark places

It was the night before Halloween when Vladimir called one last Fright Club meeting to go over **OPERATION KIDDIE SCARE.**

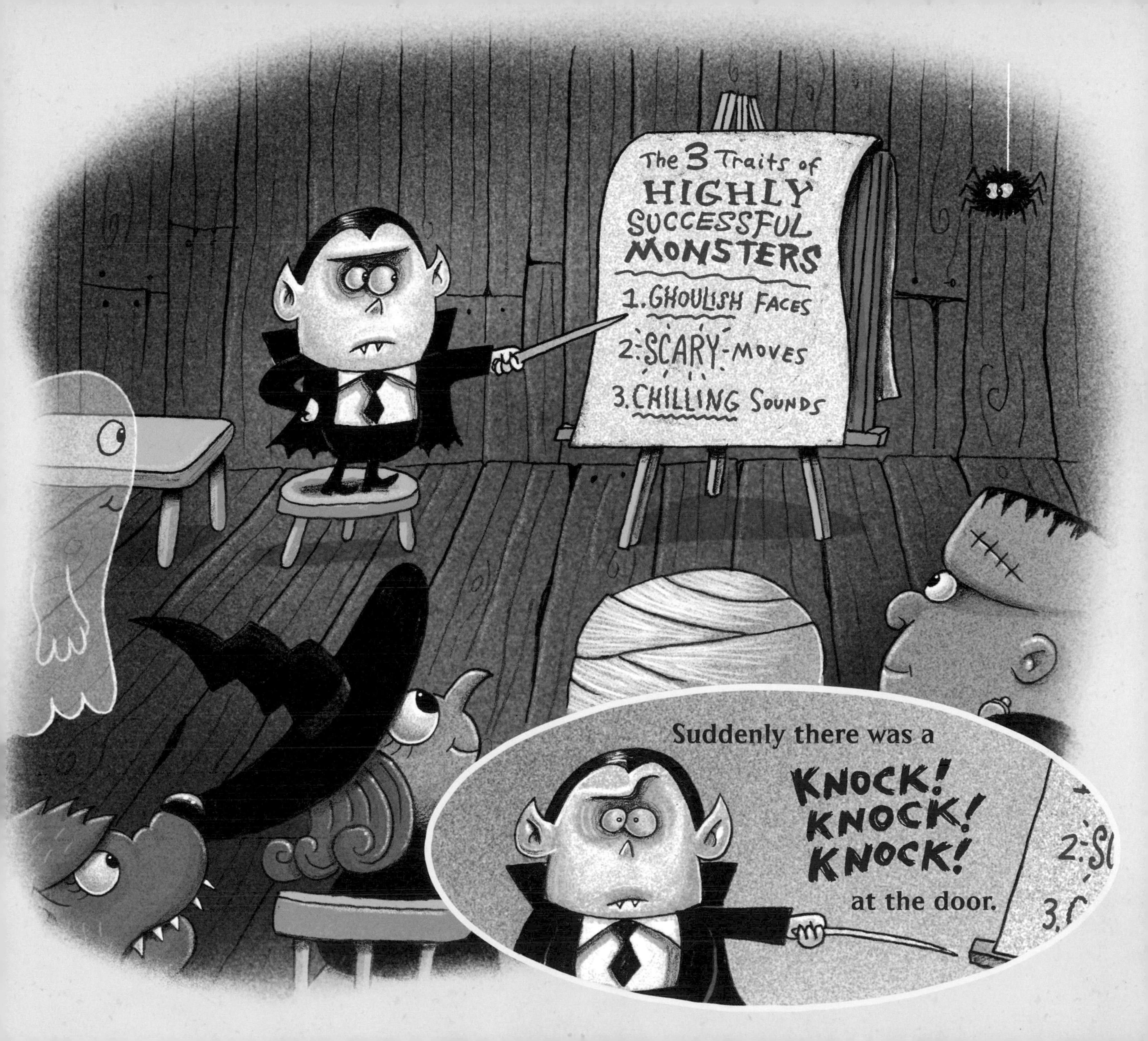

Suddenly there was a

KNOCK! KNOCK! KNOCK!

at the door.

Vladimir got back to business.

Everyone gathered around Mumford.

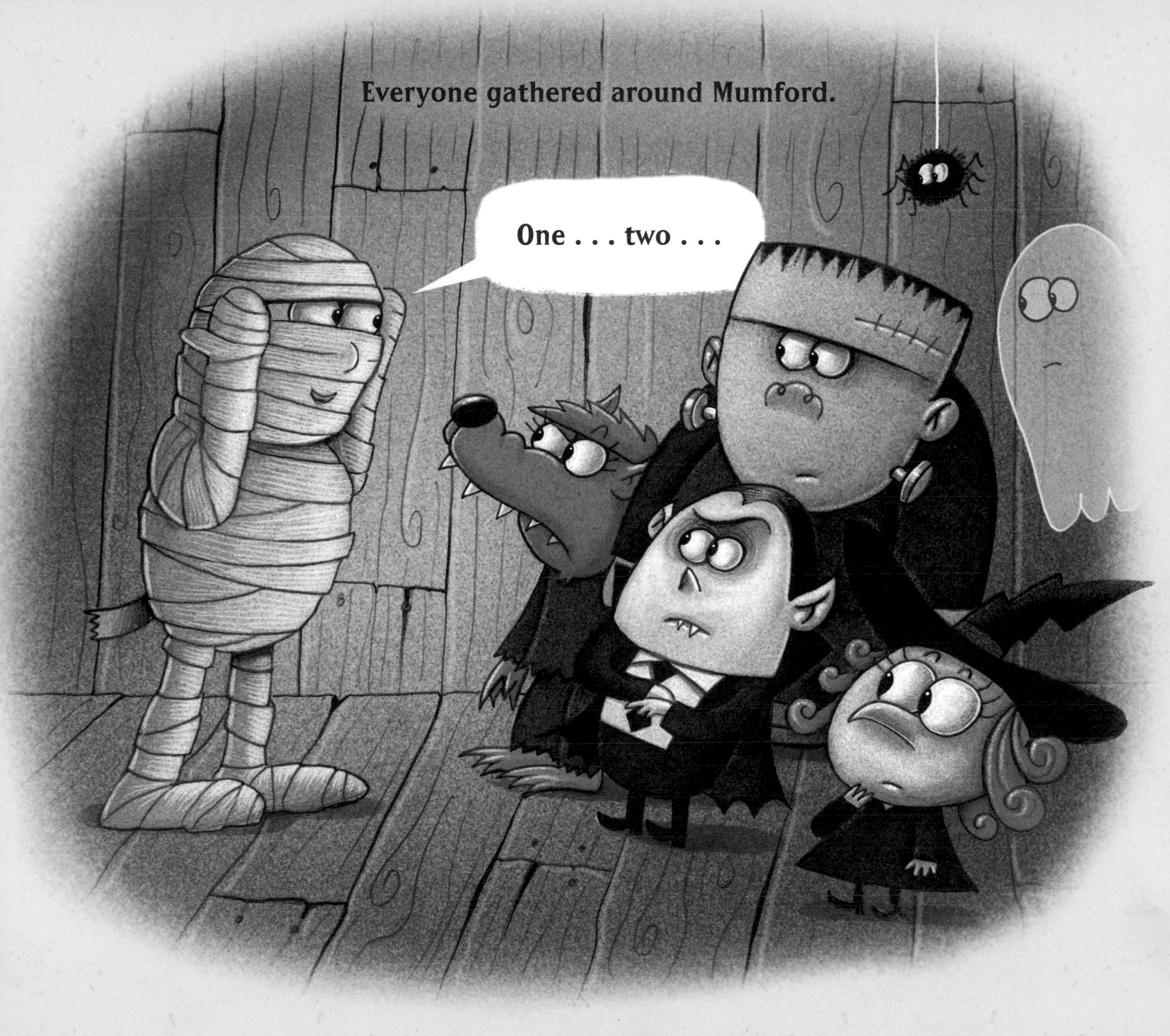

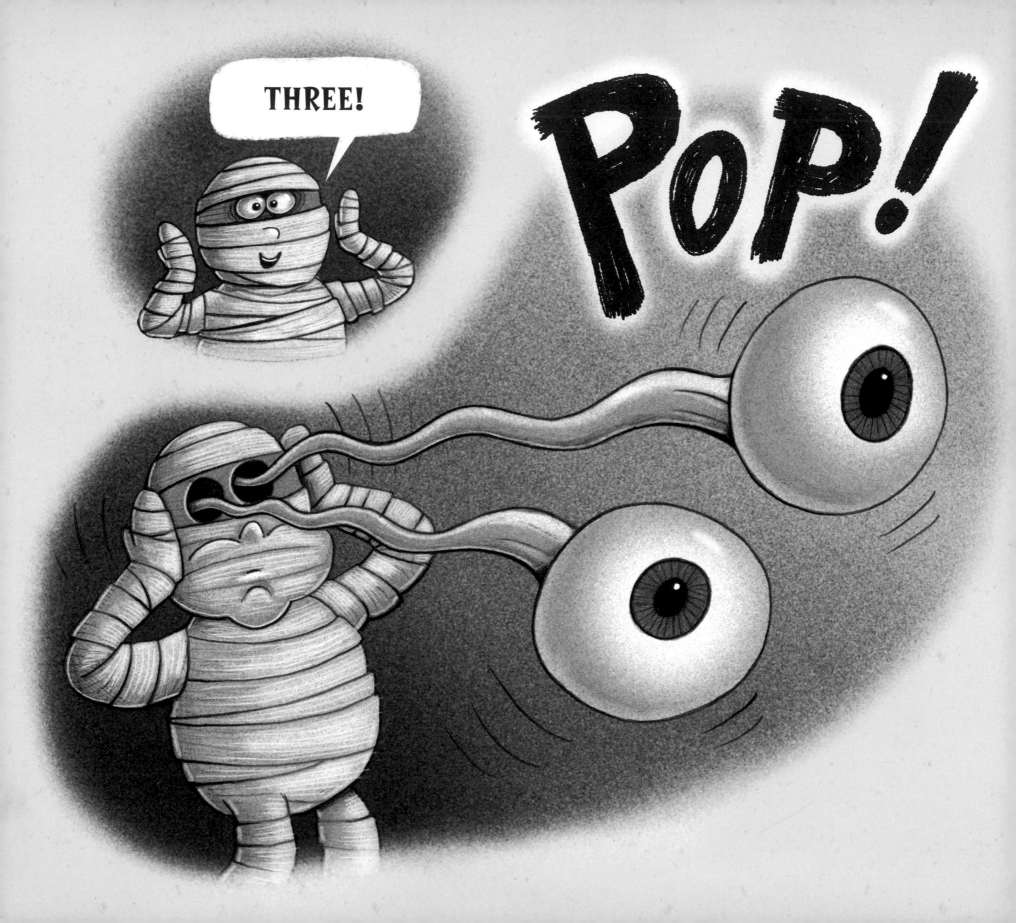

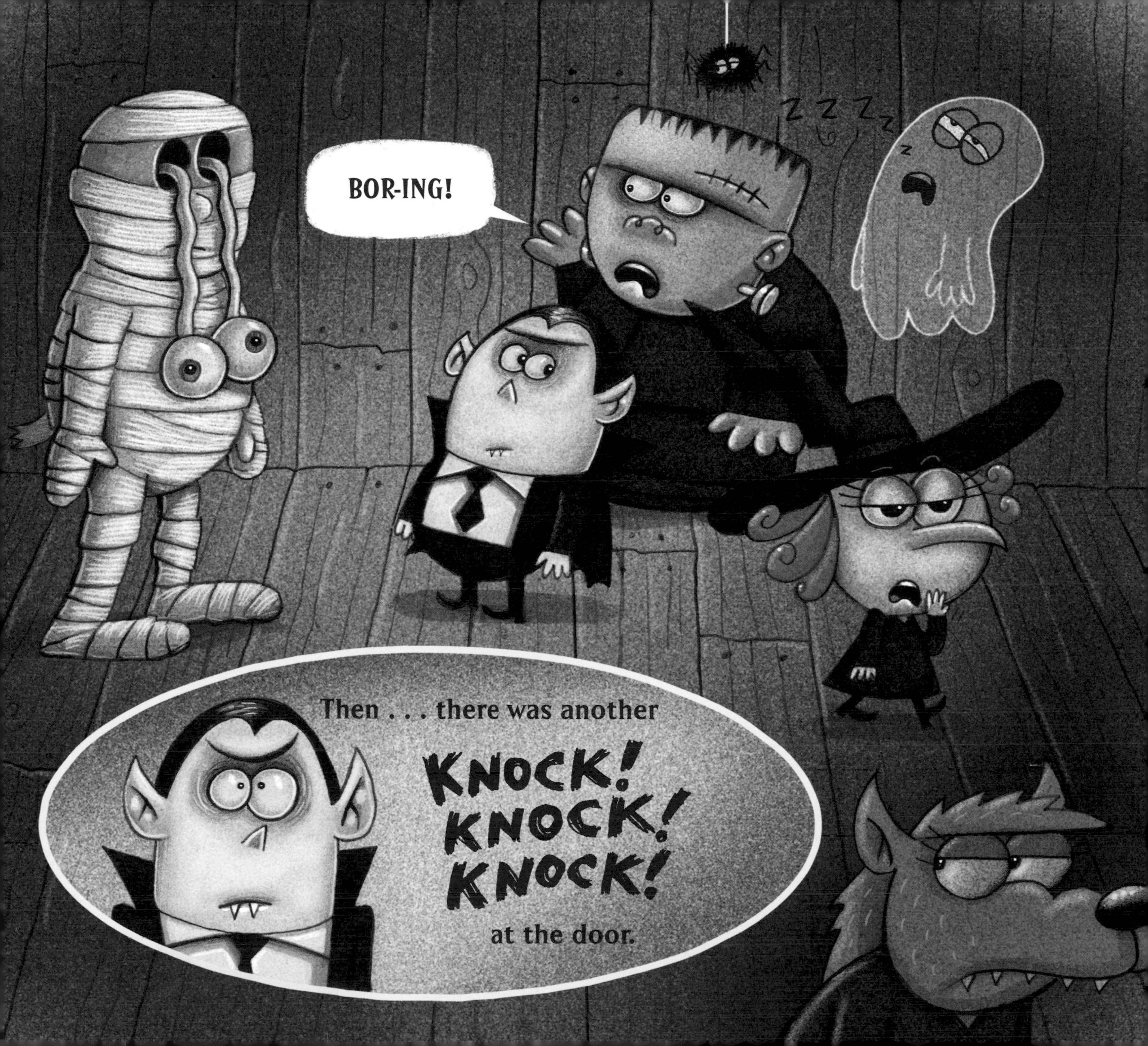

Then . . . there was another

KNOCK!
KNOCK!
KNOCK!

at the door.

Vladimir tried to refocus.

The monsters definitely had some scary moves,
but not in the way Vladimir had hoped.

BAM! BAM!
BAM!

went the door.

But the critters did NOT go away.

Turns out, not only monsters make ghoulish faces,

scary moves,

and chilling sounds.

And when it comes to scaring,
the more the merrier.

Vladimir was sure that Operation Kiddie Scare wouldn't be just good . . .

. . . it would be SCARY good!